Who's Your Friend?

Marian Iseard

Published in association with
The Basic Skills Agency

Hodder & Stoughton

A MEMBER OF T

Acknowledgements
Cover: Stuart Williams
Illustrations: Jim Eldridge

Orders; please contact Bookpoint Ltd, 39 Milton Park, Abingdon, Oxon OX14 4TD. Telephone: (44) 01235 400414, Fax: (44) 01235 400454. Lines are open from 9.00–6.00, Monday to Saturday, with a 24 hour message answering service. Email address: orders@bookpoint.co.uk

British Library Cataloguing in Publication Data
A catalogue record for this title is available from the British Library

ISBN 0 340 77611 0

First published 2000
Impression number 10 9 8 7 6 5 4 3 2 1
Year   2005 2004 2003 2002 2001 2000

Copyright © 2000 Marian Iseard

Typeset by GreenGate Publishing Services, Tonbridge, Kent.
Printed in Great Britain for Hodder and Stoughton Educational, a division of Hodder Headline Plc, 338 Euston Road, London NW1 3BH, by Atheneum Press, Gateshead, Tyne & Wear

Who's Your Friend?

Contents

1

Friends

Matt wasn't sure when it had started.
Maybe last summer when he used to go down
to the park with the others.
John, Simon and Dean.
They'd all been at school together,
but last summer they'd left.
John was working now, in his dad's shop.
Simon and Dean were on training schemes,
and so was he, Matt.
They had hardly any money,
which was why they hung around the park.

Dean was the one who'd begun it.
At school he'd had a thing
about the Asian kids.
A couple of times he got into fights.
Well, when you heard his Mum and Dad talk
you could see where he got it from.
Matt didn't get on so well with Dean,
but he was part of the group,
so he put up with him.

Still, he didn't like it when he saw Dean
picking on Asian kids in the park –
calling them names, insulting them,
making out he was going to get them later.
And then, when the others started to join in,
he felt really bad.
These were his friends –
but what they were doing wasn't right.
He knew that, but to say it was difficult.
So he kept quiet.
They were all right really, he kept telling himself.
If he could just stop them doing that,
they'd be OK. A good laugh.
Anyway, who else would he hang around with?

That was when the play had come along.

One day he got in from college
and his Dad's friend Pete was there.
He was all right, Pete.
They sometimes all went to
the football together.
Today he'd come to ask Matt something.

'Matt – how would you like to be in a play?'

Pete did a lot of acting –
he was in a local group.
Now the youth group were putting on a play.
'They'll need more lads.
It's about two rival gangs – lots of fighting.'

Matt was interested.
He'd been in some plays at school.
He'd even had a good part in one of them.
The girls used to do the boy's make-up,
and nobody cared about looking daft.

That was when he'd stopped
being so shy with girls.
Before he knew it, Matt had agreed
to go the meeting.

2

Sameera

On the night itself
Matt started to get cold feet.
He felt like backing out,
but his Dad was giving him a lift.
It was easier to go than to tell his Dad
he wasn't going.

'Have a good time,' his Dad called to him
as he got out of the car.

Once inside the hall Matt wanted to turn round
and walk straight out.
Everyone knew everyone.
They were all talking loudly and laughing.
He felt out of it.

Someone came over to him, a girl.
She was Asian with long black hair.

'Hello. Are you Matt?
Pete said you were coming tonight.
He told us to look out for you.
I'm Sameera.'
Sameera told him about the play.
It was a bit like Romeo and Juliet,
about a boy and girl in rival gangs
who fall in love.

When it was time to read the play
they asked him to read two small parts.
Just a few lines.
He seemed to do all right.

Afterwards they all had coffee and sat around.
He talked to Sameera and her friends.
They were playing music that he liked
and he started to feel good.
He was glad that he'd come.

The person who was in charge of the group
was called Liz. She came over
and asked if he'd like to be in the play.
He said yes. Just like that.

'Great,' she said. 'You can be
in one of the gangs. It's not many lines.
Is that OK?

It was OK. It was a start.

Soon they were working hard,
three nights a week.
He might not have many lines
but he had a lot to do on stage.
They were shown how to stage-fight,
with real boxing and wrestling moves.

'It has to look real,' they were told.
'So the people watching believe it.'

He learnt how to throw punches,
and duck them.
He learnt how to get someone on the ground,
and how to fall safely.
It was all down to timing,
and watching your partner carefully.

One time he did get hit
and he had a few bruises from the falls.

'I need danger money!' he said to Sameera.

She grinned.
'You'll just have to learn faster!'

He was getting to like Sameera. A lot.
She was pretty, and funny too.
She seemed to like Matt as well, at least,
she often came to sit with him.

'Shall I help you learn your lines?'
he asked her one night, trying to sound
as if it didn't matter to him.

'OK,' she said.

It was a bit boring, going over and over
the same lines, but Matt didn't care!

Some evenings a boy came along at the end
to walk Sameera home
and Matt began to feel jealous
– until he found out it was her brother.
He thought he would like to ask her out,
but he'd hate it if she said no –
having to see her every week.
Maybe he should wait until after the play.

Suddenly Matt thought of the lads.
John, Simon and Dean.
What would they think, what would they say
if he asked an Asian girl out?

He just wouldn't have to tell them.

3

Dean

The next time he saw them
they went into town.
They met at the top of the park
and walked through it.
Matt hadn't seen them for a while
and he was worried
in case they started any trouble.
He felt more and more strongly
how wrong it was –
even more so now he knew Sameera.

On the way in they were messing around,
having a laugh,
just taking the mickey out of each other.
Then they started asking him about the play.

'What's it about then?' asked John.

'About two street gangs,' he said.
'Like Romeo and Juliet, only modern.
There's some fighting in it.'

'Do they want me in it?' asked Dean.
'I'll show them how to fight.'

He punched the air and the others laughed.
Dean had often been in scraps at school,
but he hadn't always won them.

'More like how to lose a fight,' Matt joked.

'Want to bet?'

Dean punched Matt in the chest –
not really hard, but hard enough to
knock him off balance a little.

'Watch it,' Matt said,
'I know some things about fighting now.'
'You? You always stood and watched,
you were chicken.'

'Just because I didn't want to fight,
doesn't make me chicken.'

'Oh yeah? Come on then …'

Dean ran round in front of him,
and hit him again, harder this time.
Matt remembered what he'd learned.
He hooked his leg round one of Dean's,
then yanked and pulled him to the ground.
Before Dean could get up he sat on his back,
grabbed one arm
and pulled it high up behind his back.
Dean was smaller, lighter than Matt.
He was stuck underneath him.
He didn't have the strength to get Matt off.

'Get off – you're breaking my arm!'
Matt stood up.
Dean lunged at him but Matt dodged
out of the way at the last minute
and Dean landed on the ground again.
By now Simon and John
were killing themselves.

'Face it Dean, you've lost your touch,'
said John. 'Matt's cool!'

It was only a joke, but Dean's face
was red with anger.
He stood up, rubbing his arm.

'Very funny,' he muttered.
'Pity he's fighting in a poofy play,
instead of on the street.
That's what I call hard.'

Matt said nothing, but he knew Dean
would try and get him back – sometime.

4

Who's Your Friend?

Once in town the fight was forgotten.
They went round the shops.
John bought some clothes.
Simon bought some new trainers.
Matt bought a CD – it was all he could afford.

Just as they were coming out
of the record shop
Matt heard a voice he knew.

'Hello Matt!'

It was Sameera, with a friend.
She smiled at him,
as if she wanted to stop and talk.
Matt looked at the others,
who were heading for the door.

'Hi,' he said, playing it cool.

'What did you buy?' Sameera asked.

'Oh, nothing much.'

He wanted to escape.
By now the others had stopped.
They were waiting for him, watching him.

'Let's have a look. What is it?'

Sameera tried to grab the bag,
but he swung it away from her,
behind his back.
She laughed, and tried to dodge behind him.

'Come on Matt, what's the big secret?'

'Leave it,' he said. 'It's no good.
It's for my Mum.'

She gave him a funny look, but he didn't care.
He just wanted to be on his way.

'Oy! Matt!' It was Dean. 'Are you coming?
Or are you getting friendly with the enemy?'
He said it very loud and the others sniggered.

Sameera looked at Dean, then at Matt.
Her smile had gone,
and he knew what she was thinking.
But he had to go.
He didn't want to look
as if he knew her too well,
it would be just what Dean wanted.
A chance to have a go at him.

'I'll see you on Tuesday,' he said, and went.

As they walked out of the shop
Dean turned to Matt.

'Who's your friend?'

His voice had an edge to it.
Like he wanted to prove something.

'No one. She's in the play. That's all.'

Afterwards he hated himself.
Saying that,
as though Sameera meant nothing to him.
All to stop Dean knowing he was friends
with a Pakistani girl.

Maybe Dean was right.
Maybe he was chicken.

5

A Falling Out

Matt dreaded the next rehearsal,
seeing Sameera.
It was worse than he thought –
she completely ignored him.
She didn't come over to say hello.
She sat with her friends
all through the coffee break.
Matt knew he had to say something,
anything to show he was sorry,
so he waited until she was on her own.

'Sameera – I'm sorry I had to rush off
on Saturday.'

'Did you?' she said. 'I didn't notice.'

Ouch!

'Well – the others were waiting for me.'

'Are they your friends?'

Her eyes were very cool, sort of far away.
He knew his answer was important.
Not just to Sameera, but to himself.
Whatever he said, it would decide something.

'Sort of. They're old friends but …
sometimes they do things and say things
I don't like.'

'Why are you friends with them then?'

Matt shrugged.
'They're not always like that,' he said.
'They never used to be.'

She nodded.
'They sound like the sort of friends
you don't need,' she said.

Sameera turned away
and went back to the stage
and Matt had the feeling that
suddenly he had a lot to prove.

Just when he had finally decided
he wanted to ask her out.
All because of Dean.

After that, whenever he saw the others
it felt strange.
He joined in with the joking,
and the messing around,
but he felt sort of out of it.
Different.
He couldn't explain it –
like he wasn't getting the jokes anymore.

Then one Saturday afternoon
John called round.

'We're going to the fair,' he said.
'Are you coming?'

Why not? They always went together.

'OK,' he said.

6

The Fight

They met up with the others.
Dean was in a funny mood.
A bit crazy – loud, swearing a lot.
'Hey, Romeo!'
he shouted when he saw Matt.
'How's Juliet?'

He meant Sameera.
He'd never believed Matt
when he said he didn't know her.
Matt said nothing.
He changed the subject fast.

They wandered around a bit,
went on some rides.
It was busy,
the whole town seemed to be there.
Then, as they walked round the
back of the dodgems,
a boy bumped into Dean.
Just by accident.

'Sorry,' he said, and carried on.
Dean shouted after him,
'Oy, watch it – Paki.'

The boy turned, so did all his friends.

'What did you say?'

Matt stared hard at the boy's face.
He thought he'd seen him before
but he couldn't remember where.

'Watch it Dean,' Simon muttered.
'There's a few of them.'

But Dean was in an ugly mood.
'I said, go home Pakis.'

He put two fingers up at the boy.
After that everything seemed
to happen very quickly.

There was a lot of shouting
and then fists started flying.
At first it was just Dean and Simon.
Then John dived in, trying to help them out.
Matt stood back, feeling helpless.
He didn't want anything to do with this –
but if he ran off he'd never live it down.

Out of the corner of his eye
he saw two girls come running over.
One of them was Sameera.

'Leave them alone!' she was screaming.
'Leave them alone!'
Then Matt realised where he'd seen the boy.
He was Sameera's brother.

He looked at the tangle of fighting bodies,
then at Sameera.
At the same time as she saw him.
She gave him a look
that he thought he'd never forget.
Like she hated him.

By now Dean was getting the better
of Sameera's brother.
He had him pinned up against the fence,
laying into him.
Matt couldn't stand it.
He ran over and tried to pull Dean off.

'Get off him Dean, leave him!'

Dean turned and swung his fist hard.
He got Matt in the eye,
and Matt staggered backwards.
Another blow landed on his mouth,
and made him mad.
He pulled with all his force at Dean
and got him off balance,
then hit him hard. Dean fell.

If the fight hadn't been broken up then,
by some of the men who worked the fair,
Matt wasn't sure
what would have happened next.
He got taken to the entrance and slung out.
He didn't know where the others were.
He made his way home slowly.

His face was stinging
where Dean had hit him.
He put his hand up to his mouth
and saw blood on it.
He would have some explaining to do at home.
As for Sameera
there was no point even thinking
about her any more.

At least one thing was certain.
He'd had it with Dean, and the others.

7

Last Rehearsal

He'd been right about the trouble at home.
His parents had quizzed him until he told
them everything that had been going on.
He wasn't in their good books.

'At least you did the right thing
in the end,' his Dad said.
'But you should have had nothing
to do with it from the start.
You know better than that.'

Yes, he did.
But that hadn't made it any easier,
knowing what to do.

The next rehearsal was the last one.
Matt hardly dared go,
but there was no way not to.
When he turned up with a black eye
everyone wanted to know
what had happened to him.

'A bit of a fight,' he said.

'When I said practise at home
I meant your lines,
not the fighting!' Liz joked.

'Well I wanted to look right for the part,'
he said, and everyone laughed.
All except Sameera.

Later she came over to him.
'This is it,' he thought to himself,
'this is where she tells me
how much she hates me.'

'I'm sorry about your eye,' she said.
'Does it hurt?'

He couldn't believe it – *she* was sorry.

'Thank you for helping my brother.
Your friend would have really hurt him.'

'He's not my friend, or the others,'
said Matt. 'Not now.'

'I'm sorry,' she said again.

He shrugged.

'It would have happened anyway,' he said.
'They've changed. So have I.'

'Well you've got lots of friends here now.'
She smiled, and went off to get changed.

His heart felt like it was doing cartwheels!
He wanted to run after her,
ask her out there and then.

He put his hand up to his face,
and stayed where he was.
Why would she fancy him,
with a cut lip and a purple eye?
She just felt sorry for him.

8

First Night

First night! Matt had never
been so scared in his life.
Suddenly it was real,
not just having a laugh.
He had to go out on that stage.
He had to do everything just right –
in front of about a hundred people.
His family were all there,
and Gran and Grandad.
Pete was watching tonight too.

He stood at the side of the stage,
before the play started, feeling sick inside.
He was trying to go over his lines,
but thinking about fighting on stage
made him think about the fight at the fair
and Sameera.

Sameera was getting very friendly
with another guy now, called Mick.
He followed her around everywhere –
and she didn't seem to mind.
He could see them now,
on the other side of the stage,
whispering together.
Then they both disappeared.
Well, it looked like that was that,
as far as his chances went.
After this week was over
he would just have to forget about her.
Forget about everything.

'Quick, Matt, put your arm round me!'

What was this?

Sameera had grabbed his arm
and swung it round her waist.
She leaned on him,
and started whispering in his ear.

'It's Mick.
I can't stand him following me around.
I keep walking away
but he hasn't got the message.'

No, but Matt had.
She only wanted him to put Mick off –
that was all!
He started to slide his arm away.
Then he stopped and thought. Why him?
Slowly he put his arm back round her waist.

'Sameera?' She looked up at him.
'Will you go out with me one night?
When the play's finished?'

Sameera gave him a huge smile,
a smile that made him forget
all about stage fright.
'I thought you'd never ask!'